This Ladybird Book belongs to:

_____

_____

_____

Qaita

Let's read together readers and activity books are designed for you and your child to share.

Old Mother Hubbard is based on the well-known rhyme, which all children love. The rhyme is given on the left-hand page for the adult to read to the child. On the right-hand page, your child can join in by reading the text given in **bold**. Words from the rhyme are repeated, and new words are added to tell the story of an old woman and her hungry dog.

First read the book aloud. Then go through the rhyme again, this time encouraging your child to read the text on the right-hand page. The illustrations give picture cues to the words. Many young children will remember the words rather than be able to read them, but this is a normal part of learning to read. Always praise as you go along – keep your reading sessions fun, and stop if your child loses interest.

Ladybird books are widely available, but in case of difficulty may be ordered by post or telephone from:

Ladybird Books – Cash Sales Department
Littlegate Road Paignton Devon TQ3 3BE
Telephone 01803 554761

A catalogue record for this book is available from the British Library

Published by Ladybird Books Ltd Loughborough Leicestershire UK
Ladybird Books Inc Auburn Maine 04210 USA

Ladybird

Old Mother Hubbard

by Karen Bryant-Mole
illustrated by Sue King

Old Mother Hubbard
went to the cupboard...

4

Old Mother Hubbard

... to fetch the poor dog a bone.

the dog

The dog has no food.

... and so the poor dog had none.

Poor dog!

She went to the fruit shop
to buy him some fruit...

12

fruit for the dog

But when she got back
he was playing the flute.

14

The dog can play.

She went to the tailor's
to buy him a coat...

16

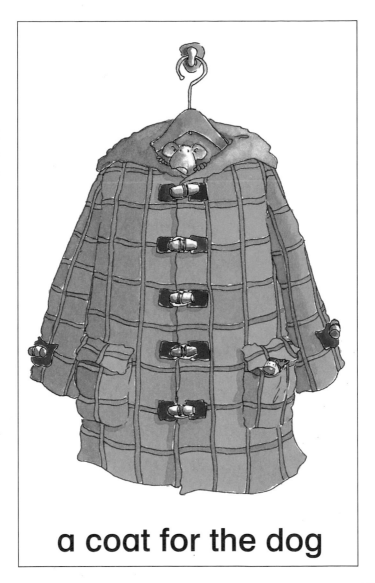

a coat for the dog

But when she got back
he was riding a goat.

The dog has fun.

She went to the cobbler's
to buy him some shoes...

20

shiny red shoes

But when she got back
he was reading the news.

The dog can read.

The dame made a curtsey,
the dog made a bow.

The dog bows.

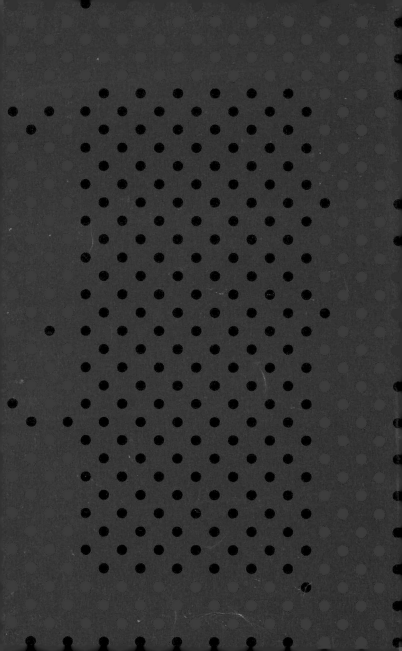